A STORY OF A GIRL AND HER NEW FRIENDS TH

WRITTEN & ILLUSTRATED
BY
SHAYANN M. HOFFER

NEELA MEETS LOTUS

The illustrations are watercolor pencil and pen. Painting images are mixed mediums

ISBN-13: 978-1494380854
ISBN-10:1494380854

Welcome,   I am glad you found us!

I would like to invite you to practice along with Neela and friends.
This is an interactive book with playful instructions and
illustrations of common yoga poses.
When you practice yoga please be gentle.
**Focus on your balance and breath. Find an open space,
comfortable attire, and Have Fun!   May love guide the way!**

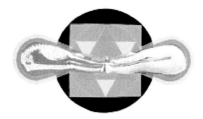

Abby~
I hope you enjoy
the book & yoga with
your sister :)
ox Shazann

"This book is dedicated to Freya, the furriest guru in my life and to all the inspiring children!" smh

अथ योगानुशासनम्॥१॥

Atha Yoganushasanam || (1-1)

Now the exposition of Yoga is being made.

Yoga Sūtras of Patañjali translated by Swami Satchidananda

"Meowwwwwwww" whispers Max the cat.
"Oh, good morning Max, looks like you want to do yoga," says Neela.

"This is a yoga pose that I like,"
Max proceeds to lift his spine reaching towards the ceiling.
"It feels good on my back," says Neela.

"Try this pose! It's called downward dog, it is my favorite," says Drew.
"This feels great all over," says Neela.

Neela, Max, and Drew decided to go outside for a walk.
"Look! There are pigeon birds on the roof,

listen to them cooo," says Neela.

All of a sudden one of the pigeons' flew down to meet Neela.
"Hi, I am Patti the Pigeon and this is my favorite pose," says Patti.
"This feels good in my hips and legs," says Neela.

Neela, Max, Drew, and Patti keep walking down the path.
"Wow, what a big, beautiful tree!" exclaims Neela.
"Why thank you. My name is Timothy the Tree," replies Timothy.

"The pose I'm most comfortable with is named after yours truly,"
says Timothy smiling. "I feel strong in this pose.
My feet are like roots in the ground," says Neela with a laugh.

Along their walk they meet another new friend.
"Well, hello there," a voice from above says.
"I'm perched peacefully. My name is Edward the Eagle."
"Hi Edward, you do look peaceful. May we join you?" Neela asks.

"Yes, this is how I stay peaceful, it's called eagle," says Edward.
Neela proceeds by crossing her arms & legs while
pressing her palms together in front of her face.
"When I stay still in this eagle pose I do feel peaceful," says Neela.

Continuing on their way,
they approach a snake in the grass.
"Hssssssssssss, what can I help you withhhhh?" says the snake.
"Greetings Sir Snake, we are on a walk and meeting new friends, what's your name?" "My name is Ssssssssssam the Ssssssssssnake, some call me Cobra," hisses Sam. "We are doing yoga today. Do you do yoga" asks Neela?

"Why of coarsssssse I do, this is called Cobra, after moi,"
Sam slithers in position.   "This feels good down my back," says Neela.
"Yesssssssssssssssssssssssssss," says Sam.

Sam brings Neela over to the near-by-pond and introduces her to his good friend Padma, the Lotus Flower.

" Padma, I'd like you to meet my new friend Neela. She likes to do yoga," says Sam.   Sam turns to Neela and tells her " Padma doesn't talk but she listens. "

Neela sits near the water like Padma.
"It's nice to meet you, you look radiant," she says.
Padma is happy to hear Neela and shines her pedals of light even more.

She bows her head and then
looks up at Padma Lotus to say,
"Thank you Padma for opening your pedals
and sharing your beauty with us!"

All of a sudden a rainbow appears up the
sky with a spectrum of light.

Neela turns to recognize all of
her new friends, smiling with bright eyes,
remembering all the new yoga poses and says

"Thank you friends, let's do this again!"

~Namaste ~

CREATE YOUR OWN MANDALA! ⟶

This is an ancient pattern found in many of the world's cultures.
The "Flower of Life" mandala consists of seven or more overlapping circles.
Traditionally mandala's are started from the middle and worked outward.
Try new shapes, play with patterns, mix different colors, add an intention.
It's limitless! *Where else do you see these shapes in nature?*

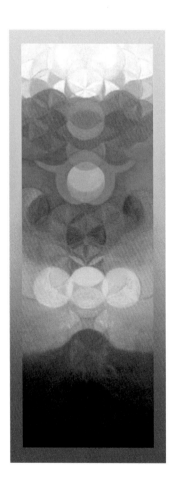

Author & Illustrator: SHAYANN M. HOFFER

"I love yoga! I love art! I love nature! I love learning!
  These are a few of my interests that make my life so full of joy!
  I want to share the joy with You." smh

Shayann is a certified yoga and art instructor.
She has been working with youth for over a decade
in artist residencies for public & private schools and
organizations. Traveling as an educator has brought
her to places like the Hawaiian Islands, Canada,
Minnesota, Oregon, and the Pudget Sound of
Washington State, where she now lives.
Yoga brings clarity and Light. Connection to all!
Empower the Children!

To learn more about Shayann go to:
www.shayann.massageplanet.com
www.mnartists.org/Shayann_Hoffer

Made in the USA
Lexington, KY
30 April 2018